Professor Sniff
and the
Lost Spring Breezes

ALEX SHEARER
Illustrated by Tony Kenyon

VICTOR GOLLANCZ
LONDON

First published in Great Britain 1996
by Victor Gollancz
An imprint of the Cassell Group
Wellington House, 125 Strand, London WC2R 0BB

A catalogue record for this book is
available from the British Library

ISBN 0 575 06279 7

Photoset in Great Britain by
Rowland Phototypesetting Limited,
Bury St Edmunds, Suffolk
Printed by
Cox and Wyman Ltd, Reading, Berkshire

96 97 98 99   10 9 8 7 6 5 4 3 2 1

To Nicholas and Kate

Prologue

Callender Hill was as calm as a mill pond. The water in the river could have been made out of glass. The weather vane stood motionless on the church spire, and there was barely enough wind in the sky to flutter a feather or to carry a spider away, and there wasn't a spring breeze in sight.

Near the middle of town, in their parents' small flat, Sam and Lorna Walker looked out of the window down into a Saturday morning. It was a very still Saturday morning. And that would have been all right, if you had very still, very calm things to do. But they had been hoping to do other things, and the winds that did not come were a great disappointment.

"Promises," said Sam.

"Promises," Lorna agreed, and she looked over to where their father sat. He tried to hide behind the newspaper, but their disappointment found him out.

"Well, it's hardly *my* fault," he said.

"It's hardly your dad's fault," their mum agreed. But then she would take his side.

"Take us sailing, someone said," Sam sighed. "Down on the lake."

"Out in his dinghy, someone said," Lorna sighed. "Promised, someone did."

"But that's promises for you."

"Made to be broken, they are."

Their father put down his paper.

"Now look, you two," he said. "If there's not enough wind for us to go sailing, well, it's hardly my fault. I don't control the weather, do I?"

"Well, who does then?" Sam asked.

"No one, as far as I can see. The weather's just the weather. It's there or it isn't," said Dad. "You get it, or you don't."

"Why don't you do something else instead?" Mum said. "As you can't go out in the dinghy."

"Yes, what else can we do?" Dad agreed.

"Well, what *I'd* really like to do—" Sam

said, "—is fly my stunt kite."

"So would I," Lorna agreed. "Fly his stunt kite."

"But Sam," Dad said, "there's no wind."

"We could try."

Dad looked to Mum for help. But he didn't get any.

"You could try," she said. "Then if you all go out, I can have a bit of time to myself."

Dad put down his newspaper and got to his feet.

"All right," he said. "We can try. Come on. Fetch the kite. And let's go to the park. I don't know. Where's the weather when you want it? It's always somewhere else."

1

Professor Sniff

"It's not been a good year for wind," Professor Sniff said. "Not at all. Here we are, with a half-empty balloon, and spring already upon us."

"We'll have to put a sign up," his assistant Oswald said, "saying spring will be a little late this year. Or rather the *wind* will be a little late this year."

"Yes," Professor Sniff said. "Quite so."

Professor Sniff went out to look at his main wind-storage balloon. He had several of them moored around the wind farm, all of different shapes and sizes, but this was the largest of all. It was tied up out by the stables, a great, enormous balloon, as big as a skyscraper when it was full. But at that moment, it lay limply on the ground, and it looked very sad and wrinkled.

"It looks like a party balloon," the professor thought, "two days after the party's over. When all the fun's gone out of it."

And it did, too. For there was a smile painted on it. And when the balloon was full, it had great fat cheeks, and its smile could be seen for miles. But now, it just looked plain miserable.

Oswald stood shaking his head.

"Folks don't understand," he said. "When there's a water shortage, they seem to get the hang of that all right. They say: 'Aye, aye, we've had no rain for a while, so I'll go a bit easy on the sprinkler.' But wind—"

"You're right, Oswald," Professor Sniff said. "People just take it for granted. They assume it'll always be there. And they go on burping and hiccuping, and using it up as if wind was a bottomless pit."

"Yes," Oswald agreed. "They never think that wind has to be kept and stored, just the same as fresh drinking water."

"And our wind is always fresh!" Professor Sniff said.

"None fresher," Oswald said. "None of that artificial rubbish."

"Best sea breezes," the professor said. "Free-range Hiccups too, if you want them. None of these factory-farmed Hiccups, but proper free-range ones, that have had a decent life." And as he spoke, he was interrupted by a loud Hiccup, which had managed to escape from the Hiccup House.

"There they go," Oswald said. "They're hatching out. I'd better go and put them in a box to keep them quiet, or we'll never hear the end of it."

Strange noises came from all over the farm, especially from the direction of the Burp Barns, where the Burps were reared in large numbers,

and the burping went on all night. Next to that was a storage shed containing several tubs of rather large and loud Belches, which had even won prizes at the county show, though it must be said, they were a bit on the fruity side. One of Professor Sniff's Belches had even won a first in its category. And he had been awarded a rosette on its behalf, which he took home, pinned to his chest. It read First Prize, Champion Belcher, Professor P. J. Sniff.

Also in the shed were some bags of Huffs, some sacks of Puffs, a few stray Whiffs, some Wheezes, and some Pants. Not the sort that you wore, of course, but the kind of pants that you had when you were out of breath.

As Oswald tended to the Hiccups, Professor Sniff went around the farm checking up on things. As he did so, he passed a large barn which had a double-thick door, with a double-thick lock on it and a double-thick chain.

The doors of the barn creaked and bulged outwards as though something ferocious were trying to get out.

"Now, now," Professor Sniff said. "Temper, temper."

But the doors creaked even more, as though at any moment they might burst open. A sign on them read:

Dangerous Hurricane. Do Not Open Under Any Circumstances. Safety Hats Must Be Worn, And Tied On With String.

Sometimes the chain on the doors rattled so loudly, it could be heard miles away in the town.

"What's that, Dad?" Lorna Walker would ask her father, when he came to say good night. "Is it monsters?"

"No," he said, "it's just the wind. Nothing

to be afraid of." Professor Sniff had picked up the hurricane on a holiday to Florida, when he was off on one of his wind-gathering expeditions. It was only a baby when he had managed to lure it into a bin-bag. He had brought it back home on the aeroplane without any of it escaping, and it was so small then, it had gone on board as hand luggage.

It was an odd-looking breeze, as breezes blow. And Professor Sniff had not easily identified it at first.

"Could be a small hurricane," he thought. "Or on the other hand, it could just be a very large sneeze."

He had almost lost it at the airport, when the customs man had said to him:

"Anything to declare? What's in that bag?"

"Just some wind," Professor Sniff said. "It's a souvenir."

"Seems a funny sort of souvenir—wind."

"I collect it," Professor Sniff said. "For my wind farm. I collect all sorts of wind from all round the world. My card."

He handed the man his card. It read:

Blow Me Down Sideways Wind Farm.
Prop. Professor P. J. Sniff.
Wind Old, New, Second-Hand and Recycled.
Burps bought and sold. Best prices paid.
Wind supplied for all occasions.
Kites, regattas, wind-surfing, etc.
Spring Breezes a speciality.

"I don't always buy and sell it though," Professor Sniff explained. "If I get very fond of a bit of wind, I might just keep it as a pet. A home's not a home without some wind around the place. Yes, we've got loads of wind in our house. Haven't you?"

"Certainly not," the customs man said. "And if we do get any, we open a window, so it all goes out."

"Ah, well, when I open a window, it all comes in, you see," the professor said. "I'm like that with wind. I attract it. I'm like a magnet for it somehow. I suppose you could say I've got wind in my veins."

And it was true that Professor Sniff was in a state of constant motion. Tiny breezes blew through his hair and tickled his nostrils, or shot up his trouser legs and back down his sleeves. The handkerchief in his top pocket rippled, and his tie flapped up and down. Even standing still, he was always on the move. At night, he had wind in his pyjamas. If he went swimming, there was wind in his trunks. And though he was quite thin, he looked rather tubby, as the breezes expanded his shirt and gave him a large stomach.

"So how much would you say this bag of wind is worth then?" the customs man asked. And he gave the baby hurricane a poke with his pencil—which it didn't much seem to like.

The professor scratched his chin.

"Difficult to say," he said. "Baby hurricanes aren't worth a lot. They don't often amount to anything. A whirl here, a whirl there, then they're finished. It's only the odd one that ever makes a name for itself."

"Like Hurricane Charlie," the customs man said, remembering a particularly nasty hurricane he had heard about on the news. He'd seen it on the television, pulling the roofs off houses, uprooting palm-trees and blowing cars off the road, as if they weighed nothing at all.

He let Professor Sniff go on his way, calling after him as he went, "I hope you'll see that hurricane never gets out. If it turns into another Hurricane Charlie, it could be dangerous."

"Don't worry," Professor Sniff called back. "It'll be all right."

Professor Sniff's wind-hand, Oswald, had never been keen on the hurricane, not even at the start.

"It's not local," he said. "And it don't belong here. Hurricanes come from different climates, and that's where they should stay. It's like bringing lions and tigers over and sticking them in safari parks. I'm not saying as they won't prosper, only they aren't in their natural habitats. And what if they escape? They'll be a danger to the public."

But Professor Sniff told Oswald not to worry, and he left the little hurricane inside the barn, intending to get a glass case for it and to put it in the living room, along with all the other exotic winds and breezes he had brought home from his trips abroad. But he just didn't seem to get round to it.

2

A Bag of Sneezes, a Box of Coughs

Yes, Professor Sniff really had meant to do *something* about the baby hurricane in the barn, but he and Oswald and Mrs Sniff were so busy with the running of the wind farm that he never seemed to find the time.

The work began early, and finished late, and there was always something yet to be done. At any moment the phone might ring, and a famous musician would be on the line saying:

"I've got to play a big concert tonight, and I just picked up my flute to practise, and I find I've clean run out of Puff."

"We'll send some round by messenger immediately!" Professor Sniff would reply. Within minutes a large bag of Fresh Puff would be dispatched.

Sometimes he received calls over the radio link from sailors out at sea.

"We're becalmed," they'd say. "We're stuck in the doldrums. The sails are hanging limp on the mast. Send us a breath of wind, and quick, or we'll never get home for tea."

Professor Sniff would climb into his aeroplane then. With a Wind Bomb strapped to the undercarriage, he and Oswald would fly out

over the sea until they found the yacht which had called them, sitting motionless in the water.

"Prepare to do your wind, Oswald!" Professor Sniff would say. "Prime the Wind Bomb."

"Wind up and ready," Oswald would say.

"Then let it rip."

"Wind away!" Oswald would shout, and

down the Wind Bomb would fall until it hit the sea. Then it would explode with an enormous "*Paarp!*" and the wind would shoot out, filling the sails of the boat, and carrying it off for miles at a tremendous rate of knots.

"Another successful mission accomplished, Oswald."

And the plane would return to base.

Yes, there were so many demands on the professor's time that it was small wonder he forgot about the baby hurricane in the barn. There were people on the phone one minute, wanting a bit of a breeze to dry the washing. There was someone from Scotland calling the next, who needed wind for his bagpipes. Then someone wanted to buy a few air bubbles for the goldfish tank. Someone else needed a decent bit of wind for their car tyres, as the sort they got at the garage kept giving them punctures.

For that was one of the best things about Professor Sniff's wind farm. The wind he supplied was "Completely natural. Free from pollution and additives. Ideal for asthma sufferers. A pure breath of fresh air."

It was a difficult job though, keeping the wind clean and getting all the Burps, Coughs and other impurities out of it. Before it went into the storage balloons, it was first filtered through charcoal, and bubbled through water, and all the car fumes and nasty smells were removed.

Professor Sniff liked to collect the wind for the storage balloons first thing in the morning, when it was at its freshest. And the best time of year to collect it was in the spring. This was when the wind harvest was at its finest, and you could gather a vintage crop.

"Those fresh spring breezes, they can't be beat," he'd say. "A cool spring breeze coming up from the meadow, people will pay a lot for that, come the long hot days of summer. Oh, I know you can buy this artificial stuff, electric fans and air-conditioning and all that business. And it's all right in its way, I'm not saying it isn't. But you don't get the quality."

Yes, those spring breezes were the best. Only, this year, where were they? They weren't just late, it seemed as though they might not arrive at all.

3

The Stunt Kite

Sam and Lorna were in the park with their father, trying to get the stunt kite to fly in the windless sky.

"If you run fast enough, Dad," Sam was saying, "you should be able to pull the kite up—wind or no wind!"

"How come," Dad asked, as he disentangled the lines, "that it's always *me* who does the running?"

"'Cause you're good at it," Lorna said.

"That's right," Sam agreed. "Here you are, Dad, I'll chuck the kite up again, so you can do a bit more, and show us how good you really are. I bet if you got into training, you could even win the Fathers' Race this year."

"I've got a better idea," Dad said. "How about this time *you* do the running, and *I* throw the kite up in the air?"

Sam looked at Lorna. Lorna looked at Sam. They shook their heads.

"No, Dad," Lorna said. "No, I don't think so. No, throwing up the kite is difficult, Dad. It's a bit too advanced for you."

"Yeah, complicated," Sam agreed. "You'd only get confused. It's a bit tricky for elderly people."

"You'd get tangled in the string, Dad, and fall over and hurt yourself."

"And Mum would only get cross with us, for not looking after you."

"No, you're too big and clumsy to throw up the kite, really, Dad."

"Best to stick to what you're good at."

"Doing the running."

"OK?"

Dad didn't look convinced, but as it was two against one, and he wasn't in a mood to argue, he went along with it.

"OK. One more try. But if it doesn't work this time, that's it!" he said.

He began to run, holding on to the lines. As he did so, Sam threw the kite up into the sky. Dad ran faster, and the kite rose up a little.

Just then, a small dog caught sight of him, and decided to follow. Dad ran faster to get away from the dog, so the dog ran faster to keep up with him.

"Keep it up, Dad, you've nearly got it flying! Another hundred yards—"

"Get that dog off!" Dad yelled. "He's after my ankles! Get that pesky dog off before I—"

And then there was a ker-thump.

"—have an accident."

Dad landed in the middle of the boundary hedge which ran along by the park railings. The kite behind him floated listlessly to the ground, as he lay there in the bushes.

"Ah, shame, Dad. Didn't work. Almost, but not quite." Sam said.

"You all right, Dad?" Lorna asked.

"I'll live," he said. And as he sat up he saw two beady eyes looking at him, about two inches away from his own. Beady eyes and a wet nose and a long pink tongue which came out and licked his glasses.

Before Dad could do anything, the dog's owner arrived.

"What's the big idea," she asked, "chasing my dog like that?"

"*He* was chasing *me*!" Dad said. "You can't chase someone when you're in *front* of them, can you."

"That's beside the point," replied the old lady. "And what are you doing to him now? Feeding him your glasses, by the look of it. Well, that's highly dangerous, trying to feed a dog your spectacles. He might swallow them, and cut himself."

"I didn't give him my glasses! He helped himself!" Dad said. "In fact, you should keep that dog under better control."

The old lady, who was called Miss Endicott, turned to Sam and Lorna:

"And you children should keep your father under better control. When I was your age, I was very strict with my parents. Many a time I had to send my father to his room, or confiscate his pocket money when he wouldn't eat his greens. Personally I'd recommend a good spanking for your father, but that's not the way these days, I know. Back when I was a girl though, we used to spank our parents regularly, and they were none the worse for it. A good spanking and a smack when they're naughty, it does them no harm at all." She looked at her dog. "Ankle, Tiddles," she said, then she hesitated. "No, I mean, heel. Yes, that's it, heel. We'd better put your lead on."

She rummaged about inside her bag for the dog's lead, and as she did so, something made a tinkling, musical sound. The more she rummaged, the more music came out of her bag, until Sam and Lorna could bear it no longer.

"What have you got in there? A piano?" asked Lorna.

"A guitar?" suggested Sam.

"A trombone?"

"No, this," said Miss Endicott. And she pulled out a set of wind chimes. "They're called—called—what are they called? Drat! My memory's gone again. I'm getting so absent-minded these days, I sometimes forget a thing as soon as I've heard it."

"I think they're called wind chimes," Dad said.

Miss Endicott stared at him for a second. "No, I don't think so," she said. "I think they're called wind chimes."

"Why have you got wind chimes in your bag?" Lorna asked. "Are they a sort of burglar alarm? Do they go off if someone steals your bag?"

"No, no, I'm taking them back to the shop," Miss Endicott said. "I only bought them yesterday. I got them home, and they don't work."

"I think that's because—" Dad began to say that the chimes probably didn't work because there wasn't any wind. But he didn't get the chance.

"Come along, Tiddles," Miss Endicott said.

"Let's be on our way, and leave this gentleman to his spectacles."

"Is he called Tiddles?" Sam said. "That's a funny name to call a dog."

"It's no funnier than calling a palace Buckingham," Miss Endicott said. "Or calling a square Trafalgar. And if you can call a frog Kermit and a tank engine Thomas, then why can't you call a dog Tiddles?"

"Because it's a cat's name, isn't it?"

"No it isn't," Miss Endicott said. "That's just what cats tell you, as they're trying to keep the name for themselves. Same as cows are trying to keep Daisy to themselves, and bears all want to be called Teddy. But you can call things what you like as far as I can see. Why can't you call a giraffe Shorty if you want to? And I've always thought that Tweetie Pie the elephant had rather a nice ring to it."

And she began to sing:

"Tweetie pie the elephant packed her trunk, And ran away from the circus—"

"I think I'm getting a headache," Dad said. And it was strange, but Miss Endicott was always giving people headaches.

"Then you should get your brains looked at," she told him. "And have them fixed as soon as possible. I'd take them down to the garage, if I were you, and get them tightened up." And with that she was off across the park, with Tiddles hurrying behind her.

"What a strange woman," Dad said. "Shall we go home?"

"One more try with the kite first, Dad?" Sam pleaded. "One more, eh? Just one?"

Tweetie pie the elephant packed her trunk, And ran away from the circus —

4

A Big Wet Slurp

Now on returning from his wind-collecting holiday in America ("one of my whirlwind tours", as he liked to call them) Professor Sniff, as we know, left the baby hurricane in the barn and promptly forgot all about it.

"Probably won't last anyway," he said. "They don't travel well. I'll have a look at it in a couple of days, and see how it's getting on. It can't do much harm, tied up there in the bin liner." And he had gone about his business.

A few days later, Oswald had been walking past the barn, carrying a bucket of swill, on his way to feed the Hiccups, when he heard a loud Pop!

He didn't think much of it at the time. Pops and parps were all part of daily life on a wind farm. But later that day, when he was putting fresh straw down for the Huffs and Puffs, he remembered the noise, and thought he ought to mention it to the professor.

Oswald found him in his office, helping Mrs Sniff to wrap up a big Sneeze.

"Rush order," the professor explained. "Someone with a peanut stuck up their nose. Don't ask me how it got there. But they need a good Sneeze to get rid of it. And this is one of the best we've got."

Mrs Sniff sealed the box with tape.

"I'll take it to the post right now," she said. "Back in a couple of gusts." And she was off in a billow of skirts.

"Yes, Oswald?" the professor asked, when she had gone. "Something I can do for you?"

"It's that baby hurricane of yours," Oswald said, "that you brought back from your holidays. I heard a big pop as I walked past the barn this morning, and I'm afraid it might have got out of the bag. I didn't like to open the door and look in, in case it escaped. But I think you ought to keep an eye on it, Professor, it being, you know, foreign. It might worm its way under the door. Then there's no telling what it might do. It might even turn spiteful."

"Very well, Oswald," the professor said. "Thank you for telling me. I'll have a look at it as soon as I can. Now, if you don't mind, I've got rather a big order to send off. A lady and a gentleman rang up to say they'd fallen in love, and could we send them some Soulful Sighs and a couple of Soppy Kisses, and I'd better get them off.

"Not that I like working with Soppy Kisses all that much, I have to say. They're liable to turn into Big Wet Slurps, if you're not careful. A quick Peck on the Cheek from your granny, I don't mind at all, because you can rub that off in no time. But a Big Wet Slurp, well, you need the hair dryer for one of them. And a towel."

So Oswald went back to work and left the professor to deal with the baby hurricane. And once again he promptly forgot all about it.

Now Big Wet Slurps and Soppy Kisses were things that Sam and Lorna Walker knew about only too well, for they had a Great Aunt Hilda, who came to visit them once a year, and she always brought them with her.

"Ah, look at my little darlings!" she would cry when she arrived. "See how big you're getting. But you're not too big for a Peck on the Cheek, are you?"

Only it never was a Peck on the Cheek, as Great Aunt Hilda never had her false teeth in. It was always a Big Wet Slurp—the kind of Big Wet Slurp you had nightmares about, and which made you wake up screaming:

"Ahhh! The Big Wet Slurps are coming to get me!"

"I think Big Wet Slurps should be banned," Sam said to Lorna. "I don't think it's right that you should give Big Wet Slurps to children. I think you should give them money and chocolate and gift vouchers instead."

And Lorna quite agreed.

A week later, as he walked by the barn, Professor Sniff heard some heavy thumps coming from inside. He remembered then what Oswald had told him about the hurricane getting out of the bag, and went to investigate.

Instead of opening the door, he went to the window of the barn, wiped away the grime, and peered inside.

"Oh dear!" he said. "It's not quite what I thought. It's not a hurricane any more, it's grown into a typhoon! This is just a bit worrying indeed."

And what he saw filled him with disquiet. First he saw the remnants of the torn bin liner on the floor. Then some invisible power snatched it up, span it around, threw it up to the roof of the barn, and then dropped it again. The professor put his eyes closer to the window, and shielded his gaze from the light. He couldn't exactly see the typhoon itself, but he could chart its progress from the dust and straw it picked up and dropped as it swirled angrily around the barn.

"Good heavens! "It's looking for a way out. Oswald!" he cried. "Come here at once!"

Oswald came in a hurry, all covered in Soppy Kisses which Rowena, his fiancée, had slipped into his lunch box.

"What's up, Professor?" he said. "Have the Hiccups got out? Or have the Coughs turned nasty again? Shall I get the medicine?"

"No, Oswald, not that. It's in there. That baby hurricane's growing into a typhoon. It's getting bigger and trying to escape. We'd better double-lock the barn, and stop up all the cracks."

So they did. And it took them all morning and half the afternoon.

"There," Oswald said. "That should hold it. Only what I don't understand is how come it's been getting bigger?"

"I'm not sure," said the professor. "It must be drawing air in from somewhere. Let's hope we've sealed up all the cracks. If it sucks any more air in, and gets even bigger, well—"

"Yes, and what if it gets out?" Oswald asked.

"Untold havoc," the professor said. "And wholesale destruction."

"Can't say as I like the sound of that much," Oswald said. "Not wholesale haddock and unsold reductions. It sounds a bit nasty."

"Yes," said Professor Sniff. "Let's just keep it locked up, and keep an eye on it. It'll die off soon. Winds always do. They don't last for ever. It'll whirl itself into exhaustion, and shrivel up from lack of nourishment. Yes, it'll die off in a couple of days now. Mark my words."

But if Oswald had marked his words, he wouldn't have given him very good grades for them. For the professor was quite wrong. The typhoon didn't even begin to die off in a couple of days.

It just got bigger.

And Bigger!

And BIGGER!!

"I don't know what it's eating," Oswald said, "to get so big. But it's definitely eating something."

5

Wind Not Included

When Miss Endicott left the park, leaving Sam and Lorna and their dad behind—still trying to get their kite to fly in the windless air—she and Tiddles the dog made their way along to the High Street.

Once there, they headed for Stribberlings, a large and rather posh department store. It even had a doorman standing outside. He wore a grey uniform and a peaked cap, and he stood touching his cap and holding the door open for customers, and smiling at them as they went in and out.

But when he saw Miss Endicott coming, he didn't smile, he went white.

"Oh no," he muttered. "It's her again."

"Good morning," Miss Endicott said cheerfully.

"No dogs!" the doorman said.

"No dogs what?" she asked. "Is it a riddle?"

"I mean no dogs in the store," the doorman said, "unless they're guide dogs."

"Why not?"

"Rules. And rules is rules."

"Of course they are," Miss Endicott said. "What else would they be—turnips? Only you shouldn't say rules is rules. You should say rules are rules. Not rules is rules. Saying rules is rules, well, it ain't grammatical! Are it?"

"The rules say that you can only take a dog into the store if your eyesight's poor and you might bump into something," the doorman insisted. "I told you all this the last time you was here—were here."

"Well, my memory's poor," said Miss Endicott, "So I'd better take him in then, in case I forget something. He's a memory dog, you see. Guide dogs help people whose eyes are bad, and memory dogs help people whose memories are bad."

"How can a dog possibly help your memory?"

"He jogs my elbow," Miss Endicott said.

"Or if I get really forgetful, he bites my bottom—quite gently—more of a chew, really."

"Yes but—"

But it was too late. Miss Endicott and Tiddles were already inside and heading down to the gardening section in the basement.

Miss Endicott approached an assistant, who was busy arranging a display of compost.

"Excuse me!" she said. "I have a complaint. And it isn't measles."

The assistant turned. His smile vanished as soon as he saw Tiddles.

"Dogs aren't allowed," he said.

"Dogs aren't allowed what?" Miss Endicott said. "Chewing gum, you mean? Absolutely right. I never give it to him. He's fond of milkshakes, but chewing gum is out of the question. It sticks his barks together and it goes all over his paws. No, you're quite right. You should never give a dog chewing gum. Bones and milkshakes are what they like. And ice lollies when it's hot."

"No, I mean—"

But Miss Endicott didn't give him a chance.

She put down her bag and took out the set of wind chimes.

"I bought these yesterday," she said. "From this department. Wind chimes, you see. I've still got the receipt. And the box. Now, look at that box, you see what that says?"

"'Tinkle-Tinkle Wind Chimes. For A Tuneful Tinkle In Your Garden'," the assistant read out. "'Hang on the branch of a tree for best results'."

"Exactly," Miss Endicott said. "Well, I hung them up on the tree in my garden, just as it says in there. And what did I get?"

"Tinkle, tinkle, tinkle?" the assistant asked.

"No, total silence! Not a dicky bird! Not even a dicky tinkle. Just dicky nothing, that was all I got. Well, I'm not paying good money for dicky nothing, am I? That would be dicky stupid, wouldn't it?"

"Woof!" Tiddles said, in agreement. He may even have said "Dicky woof." But you'd need to have been a dog yourself to know.

"One moment," the assistant said. "If I may." He took the wind chimes, held them up, and shook them.

Tinkle, tinkle, tinkle, they went. And then *tinkle* again.

"They seem all right to me," he said.

"That's because you shook them," Miss Endicott pointed out. "Of course they work when you shake them. But they're *wind* chimes, aren't they? Not *stand there all day and shake them yourself* chimes. I can't be doing that, can I? Standing about in the garden all day shaking my chimes—whatever would the neighbours think? And my arms would get tired."

"Woof," Tiddles agreed.

"Yes, but madam, the reason they're not chiming at the moment," the assistant said, "is because there isn't any wind. It's the calmest spring on record for years, since records were invented. And not just records, since pianos were invented too."

"But surely," Miss Endicott said, "the wind should be *supplied*!"

"Beg pardon?" the assistant said.

"The wind," Miss Endicott said, "should be supplied. Look at that box. 'Tinkle-Tinkle Wind Chimes', it says. Where does it say 'Wind not included'?"

"Beg pardon again?" the assistant said.

"Doesn't say it, does it? If you buy a toy, it says on the box 'Battery not included'. Well, wind chimes should be the same. If the wind's not included, you should say so on the box. If I'd known that I was expected to provide my own wind, I'd never have bought those chimes in the first place!"

"Yes, but—" the assistant said.

"But nothing!" retorted Miss Endicott. "Look at me, I'm an elderly lady with a bad—bad—what is it you call it again?" Tiddles jogged her elbow. "Oh yes, a bad memory! I can't be expected to go providing my own wind, can I? Not at my time of life."

"But madam," the assistant said, "Stribberlings can scarcely be held responsible for any natural shortage of wind. Why, we also sell lawn-mowers. But we never say to people that they will have to supply their own grass. We somehow expect that they'll know that."

Miss Endicott looked quite shocked.

"You mean you don't supply grass with the lawn-mowers? Disgusting! And I always thought you played fair with your customers. I'm starting to think that you're nothing but crooks. I think it's a disgraceful swindle. But I don't want to argue with you, so very well, I'll buy some wind for the wind chimes. And none of your cheap stuff, mind. I want the quality wind, with a nice ring to it. The sort of wind you'd bring out if the vicar called."

"I'm afraid we don't sell it, madam. You'd need to go to a specialist dealer. I suggest you look in the Yellow Pages. Or if you wish to return the wind chimes, in view of the misunderstanding, we will be happy to give you a full refund."

"No, that's all right, thank you," Miss Endicott said. "I'll hang on to them for now. There's got to be a bit of wind somewhere. Come along, Tiddles, let's go to—wherever we're going. And a good day to you, young lady!" she said to the shop assistant.

"Young man," the assistant said.

"No, he isn't," Miss Endicott said. "He's a dog."

"Woof," said Tiddles, who didn't know what else to say, and really had very limited conversation. And he gave Miss Endicott's bottom a wondering look, as if he was unsure whether he ought to bite it or not. Or maybe give it a little chew. But he wisely decided against it.

6

Sheik Kebabs

It was Oswald who first noticed that things weren't quite right the day it all happened.

He and Professor Sniff had been working that morning on a particularly large Belch. It was to be shipped abroad in a container to a rich man in Arabia called Sheik Kebabs.

Sheik Kebabs was a regular customer, and he spent a lot of money on wind-farm produce.

"That Kebabs," Professor Sniff used to say, "he's our bread and butter."

The sheik was a nomad, which meant that he travelled around a lot, and he lived in a tent in the desert. But the sheik's tent was bigger than most people's houses, and he gave great dinner parties in it, sometimes inviting as many as two hundred people round to eat.

When the feast was over, the custom in that part of the desert was to give an enormous belch, as a sign of appreciation. In our part of the world, belching is considered to be very bad manners. But with the sheik, it was just the opposite. It was bad manners *not* to belch. And often the Sheik would turn to his son, Junior Kebabs, and say:

"Why haven't you belched, you rude and shameless boy? Show your mother that you enjoyed the lovely dinner she cooked. I don't believe you belched once, all through the first course. It's sheer bad manners!"

"Don't want to belch," Junior Kebabs would say, for he was a wilful and difficult son.

"You bad boy. Even the camel's got better manners than you! Give a good belch at once, and do some wind too, while you're at it!"

"Shan't," Junior Kebabs would say. "Don't want to."

And the stubborn boy would be sent to his tent, and he would have to stay there until he agreed to do a little belch to please his father.

When Sheik Kebabs gave a dinner party, his guests would try to outdo one another, by belching as loudly as they could, and the one who belched the loudest would be considered to have the nicest manners.

The sheik himself always tried to win this competition, but as he was a rather small man, he was not able to belch very loudly, though he did his best. But you cannot get a big bang from a small drum, and that's all there is to it.

He happened then to run into Professor Sniff, who was out in the desert on one of his wind-collecting expeditions. The sheik explained his problem, and the professor said: "Just leave it to me."

So when he got home, the professor sent him a large Belch, with his compliments. All the sheik had to do then was to hide it under his robes and stick a pin in it when he wanted it to go off, and he would have the loudest belch of all. The sheik tried it, and it was a resounding success. And the professor had supplied him with Belches ever since.

Oswald and the professor had spent the morning crating up Belches to send to the sheik for his next dinner party. Once they were done, the professor loaded the crate on to a trailer, and drove off to the station.

"I'll tidy up here," Oswald had said, "while you're away."

Oswald took his broom and went round the wind farm, sweeping up the stray Gusts, and the annoying little Draughts which got up your trousers.

But funnily, there weren't as many as usual.

"Odd," thought Oswald. "There's usually at least six bags' worth of Gusts to sweep up of a morning. Wonder where they've all gone."

As he was wondering, he saw a small Draught make its way across the farmyard, kicking up dust as it went. It went on past the Hiccup House and seemed to be heading for the Sniff Shed, but as it passed the big barn, it stopped, wavered, wobbled a bit, then changed direction and—whoosh!

It disappeared into the barn.

"Now why," thought Oswald, "did it do that?"

As he watched, he saw that all the other stray Draughts and Sniffles did the same thing. They all vanished into the barn, as if they couldn't help themselves. As if some strange and mysterious force were drawing them in.

Treading carefully, Oswald went round to the side of the barn. He stood on tiptoe, peeked in, and there was the typhoon. And far from being a baby, it was now a great monster. So big, in fact, that it was bent double, and it banged and crashed against the walls and doors in an effort to get out.

"Aye, aye!" said Oswald. "There's trouble here. I wonder how it got so big? We stopped all the cracks up."

Then Oswald thought of the draughts being sucked in under the door, and realized that the stopping-up hadn't been good enough. And he thought of the missing spring breezes, which should have arrived a week ago, but which had vanished without trace.

"I know where they've gone!" he said. "They're in there! That typhoon's grabbed them, and he's made them his own! You've got them, haven't you?!"

In reply, the typhoon growled, and lifted the whole barn a good two feet off the ground, and dropped it back down again with a thump.

"Oh dear," said Oswald, "I'd better tell the professor, as soon as he gets back."

When Professor Sniff returned, he found Oswald waiting for him.

"I reckon I might have found the spring breezes, Professor," he said.

"You have? That's marvellous! Let's get at them and bag them up!"

"No, it's not marvellous," said Oswald. "Not at all. You'd better come and see why."

He led the way over to the barn, and the professor looked in through the window.

"Good heavens!" he said, when he saw what the baby hurricane had grown into. "It's a great typhoon."

"Gigantic," Oswald said. "And how much longer will the barn hold? I told you, Professor, all these funny winds from foreign parts, you shouldn't go bringing them into the country."

"But how did it get so big?" Professor Sniff wondered.

"It's the spring breezes," Oswald said. "It's

got them in there. It sucked them in, all sneaky like, as they were going past the door. That typhoon's made them part of itself, and it's getting stronger by the minute. I don't know how we're going to keep the lid on it. That door's already bulging like a hippo's bottom. What if it breaks?!"

The professor looked grave.

"We're going to have to do something, Oswald."

"And quick," Oswald said.

"Leave it with me," Professor Sniff said. "I'll put my thinking cap on. And my thinking socks, and my thinking trousers as well."

"Right you are, Professor. If anyone can come up with a solution, you can."

But for the first time in his life, Professor Sniff was stumped. And his thinking cap and his thinking socks just didn't seem to work, and he blamed Mrs Sniff for giving them too long in the washing machine, and for washing all of the thinking out of them. He lay awake all night, worrying what to do about the typhoon. Finally he decided that, if nothing else, he should at least give it a name.

"That's it," he thought. "I'll call it Trevor. Typhoon Trevor." And at last he fell asleep.

The next day was Saturday. And this was the day that found Sam and Lorna in the park trying to fly their kite, and Mrs Endicott and Tiddles at Stribberlings department store, complaining about the lack of wind.

After leaving the shop, Miss Endicott took her wind chimes home and hung them on a branch of the tree in her small back garden, then she went in and put on the kettle for a cup of tea.

Saturday was Oswald's half day. He worked only until twelve o'clock and then he went to watch the football. So at five to twelve, he was packing up his things to go when he heard the most tremendous racket.

CREEEEAAAAKKKKK!

He stopped and turned. The noise had come from the direction of the big barn. The great double doors lay in pieces on the ground, and a huge spiral of swirling wind danced among the splinters. The wind was like a great, whirling corkscrew, over a hundred feet tall, and it looked down on Oswald as though he were no more than an insect.

Oswald's mouth fell open. A passing Gulp, which happened to be bouncing across the farmyard, saw its chance and hopped in. Oswald gulped the Gulp, and then he turned and ran towards the house.

"Professor!" he shouted. "It's got out!" And he didn't dare to look back, in case the great whirlwind was following. He got to the house and hammered on the kitchen door.

"Professor, Professor!" he yelled. "The typhoon! He's got out! And he's in a bad mood! Look!"

The professor ran outside, just in time to see Typhoon Trevor pick up one of the little wooden Hiccup Houses, where half a dozen families of Hiccups were nesting. He sucked it up into his swirling winds, drew it up to fifty feet or more above ground, and then threw it down.

Craaaaash! The Hiccup House broke into a thousand pieces.

"Hiccup, hiccup," the poor dazed Hiccups went, as battered, bruised and dented, they

staggered from the debris. Some were so badly twisted that they couldn't even go "Hiccup, hiccup" any more, and just went "Cuphic, cuphic" or "Stickup, stickup" instead.

"Quick, Oswald," the professor said. "The first-aid kit! Get those Hiccups bandaged up and give them mouth-to-mouth while—"

But before he could finish, Typhoon Trevor twisted and swirled, and with a great roar, he zoomed out of the farmyard and disappeared over the fields.

"Trevor!" the professor shouted. "Come back here at once! You're a very naughty typhoon!"

Trevor paid no attention. But he must have heard the professor, because he stopped in a nearby beetroot field, and he uprooted all the beetroot, and hurled them back towards the wind farm. Luckily they fell short. But his next attempt, with a field full of cabbages, proved more successful. One cabbage landed smack bang on the professor's head, and another sailed straight through the open farmhouse kitchen window.

"What's the idea?" Mrs Sniff said, who was

in the kitchen at the time. "I never ordered no cabbage! And certainly not through the window."

"Quick, Oswald, get the truck," the professor said. "We must go after him!"

"But it's my half day," Oswald said. "I'll miss the football."

"If that typhoon gets to town, there won't be any football, Oswald. We'll be lucky if there's still a stadium! He's got to be stopped! Before he goes on the rampage!"

"Looks to me," Oswald said, looking at the scattered beetroot and at the bruised and bashed Hiccups, "that he's gone on it

already. And besides, how do you stop a typhoon?"

"Don't worry," the professor said. "I have a plan."

7

On the Rampage

Lorna and Sam were still in the park, but Dad was sneakily trying to get them away. Every time he ran with the kite, he stopped a bit nearer to the gate, so as to be closer to getting home.

"One last time, Dad," Sam said. "One very last time."

"You said it was the very last time the last time—you said," Dad said.

"Well, I mean it this time."

"You said that you meant it last time."

"Yes, but I really mean it this time."

"All right," Dad said wearily. "One more go then. And that's it. And I really mean it this time."

"But you said you really meant it last time, Dad," Lorna said.

"Well, I do! Dad said. "So come on."

For one very, very last time then, and really, really meaning it, Dad took the lines of the kite and ran with them while Sam threw it up into the air.

The kite looked as though it was going to float idly back down to earth again, just as it had done all morning, when suddenly—

"Look," called Lorna, "it's going up!"

And sure enough, a sudden gust filled the kite, and it rose into the sky. Blades of grass trembled. The branches of the trees began to sway. Some old sweet papers and crisp bags were blown out of a litter bin. The pages of a newspaper sailed up into the air.

"Steady!" Dad shouted, pulling at the kite. "Quite a stiff breeze, this. Where did it come from? It's tugging a bit. I don't know if I'll be able to—"

"Hold on to it, Dad! I don't want to lose my kite."

Then Lorna saw it. It came down Dean Road at first, in a cascade of rubbish and litter, churning it all around, like washing in a tumble dryer. Luckily the traffic lights were on green, and so the typhoon didn't have to stop.

Though whether it would have stopped even had they been on red was another matter.

It passed by a cyclist and sucked him off his bike. It span him up into the air, and then threw him into the duck pond, where he landed with a big splash.

"What hit me?" he said. "Good job I was wearing my helmet."

"Dad," said Lorna. "Something's coming. I don't like the look of it."

"Sorry?" Dad asked. "What do you mean?"

"That!" she yelled. "There!"

Dad turned and saw it coming.

"Run!" he shouted. "As fast as you can."

They didn't need telling twice. Typhoon Trevor entered the park by the west gate. Lorna headed north, Sam went south, but Dad didn't seem to know what he was doing, and ran round in circles. He later denied that he had panicked, and said that he had just been trying to get the typhoon confused.

But Trevor headed straight for him. Maybe it was the kite that did it. Perhaps a kite to a typhoon is like a red rag to a bull. But whether it angered him, or whether he just liked the look of it, either way Trevor headed straight for it and for Dad.

"Clear off!" Dad shouted. "Go away! I'm a family man with responsibilities! We don't have typhoons in this country. You've come to the wrong place! Hop it!"

"Hang on to my kite, won't you, Dad?!" Sam called, from his hiding place under a bush. "Don't lose it!"

"Be careful, Dad," Lorna yelled. "Please don't get hurt. You haven't given us our pocket money yet!"

Before Dad could reply, the typhoon was on him. It whipped the stunt kite up into the air, and up Dad went with it, hanging on with both hands. He did a complete somersault and a back flip.

"Terrific stunts, Dad!" Lorna shouted, from under the tree where she had taken shelter. "Do some more!"

"Yeah, great stunts, Dad!" Sam agreed. "Fantastic. Again!"

Dad needed no encouragement. He span round and round like a Catherine wheel on bonfire night, going so fast he became a blur.

Then, as suddenly as it had picked him up, the typhoon dropped him. Dad fell from the sky, down through the branches of a conifer tree, to come to rest, shocked but unhurt, on a branch near the bottom. Lorna and Sam ran to congratulate him.

"Terrific, Dad. I thought that usually the kite did the stunts, but you were better. Could you do it again, Dad?"

"No," said Dad, "I don't think so. That is, I'd rather not."

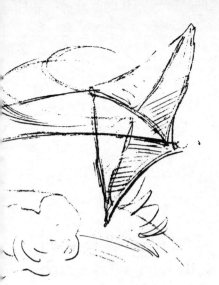

"What was that thing anyway, Dad? That wind?"

"I think," he said, "it was a typhoon. Only we don't have them here. At least we didn't once. But these days, what with all the global warming—"

"Here," said Sam, making a cross face as he examined his kite. "You've bent one of my struts."

But Dad didn't seem too interested in Sam's bent struts. He seemed more worried about his own.

8

Trevor the Menace

"But *how* do we catch it, Professor?" Oswald said. "And what *with*? And even if we *do* catch it, what are we going to *put* it in? Typhoon hunting seems a dodgy game to me."

"First of all," Professor Sniff said, "what we need is a large funnel."

He crossed the yard to where the farm machinery was kept. An old grain silo lay there, in three pieces on the ground.

"Get the bottom bit, Oswald," he said, "and let's load it on to the trailer."

The silo was a big container, once used for storing corn, and the bottom section was shaped like a funnel. Oswald and the professor loaded this on to the trailer, tied it securely, and hitched the trailer up to the truck.

"We need an old milk churn!" the professor said. "Be sure it has a lid. And get some rope."

Oswald found an old milk churn behind the dairy, where the pedigree Moos were kept. He opened the lid and peered inside to make sure it was empty. As he did, a large Hacking Cough flew out, barked at him, and hurried off.

"Coughs and sneezes spread diseases," Oswald said. "Catch them in your hanky." He made a grab for the Cough, and tried to nab it in his hanky. Too late, it was gone.

"Never mind," Professor Sniff said. "Let's get into town and after Typhoon Trevor, before he causes any damage."

"Any *more* damage!" Oswald said.

"Yes," the professor agreed. "As you say."

They got into the truck, with Oswald at the wheel. He started up the engine and off they went towards Callender Hill.

"I can see it, Professor!" Oswald said, as they drove over the brow of the hill. "There he is! Right there!"

The town lay before them. Trevor could clearly be seen from miles away. He left clouds of dust behind him, the way old steam trains once left puffs of smoke. And you could tell where he was heading by where he'd been. He was just leaving the park now, whipping up dust and litter as he went. He went down Bradwell Road, tearing up lawns and hedges.

Cats went flying in all directions, and pigeons ran for cover. The paper boy lost all his newspapers. The typhoon passed the milkman, and sucked all the milk clean out of his bottles, so that all he was left with were empties.

"Oi!" the milkman said. "Bring that milk back! It's not paid for!" But Trevor was long gone. He turned left at the bottom of the street, and headed for Acacia Avenue—where Miss Endicott lived.

Miss Endicott was in her sitting room. Tiddles was at her feet, and Fido, her cat, was on her lap, as she sat writing a letter to the chairman of Stribberlings department store.

"Dear Sir," she wrote. "I bought a set of wind chimes from your store only the other day, and you can imagine my surprise when—"

And then she heard something.

At first it was just a quiet tinkle.

"Ah," she said. "It seems the spring breezes are here at last, Tiddles. I must go and hang the washing out. But before I do that, I must wash it. Or maybe, just for a change, I'll hang it out first and then I'll wash it after."

But when she looked for Tiddles, he was hiding under the sofa. And Fido was under there with him.

"What's the matter with you two?" she said. "You're surely not afraid of a bit of wind."

Then, out in the garden, there was a loud creak, a sudden mighty *Plop!* and Mrs Endicott's wind chimes, together with the tree they were tied to, simply vanished, sucked up into the air by Typhoon Trevor. And there was nothing left in the garden but a big, gaping hole.

"Good heavens!" Miss Endicott said. "Someone's pinched my tree! I must ring the police immediately! It's daylight robbery! Daylight garden robbery! It's tree robbery! Stop! Bring it back. Stop, thief!"

As Miss Endicott stared into the sky, watching her tree vanish into the distance, Sam and Lorna Walker took their dad home. He looked blown about and battered, and had an awful lot of pine needles sticking in him. When they got him home, their mother took one glance at him and said, "What have you been doing

with your father? He looks like he fell out of a tree."

"I did," Dad said.

"He makes a great stunt kite, though," Lorna said. "Perhaps we can go out later and fly him again."

Oswald and the professor drove on into town, keeping Typhoon Trevor in view. They only had to follow the damage: the roof tiles, the upturned cars, the broken chimney-pots and the scattered washing. They even found a sea-gull waddling across the road with all its feathers blown off.

"Wheresmefeathers!" the bird squawked. "Wheresmefeathers!" Oswald gave it a paper bag to wear until they grew back again.

"Thanksabunch!" it squawked. "Thanksabunch!" And being unable to fly again until its feathers grew back, it went off in search of a bus stop.

"That Trevor," Professor Sniff said, "is a menace."

Miss Endicott picked up her telephone and rang the police station. The telephone lines to her house were still working, although Typhoon Trevor had blown several other lines down. At that moment he was in the supermarket car park, having fun with the trolleys.

It was Sergeant Porter who answered Miss Endicott's call.

"I wish to report a theft," she said. "Someone's pinched my tree."

"Your tree?" Sergeant Porter said. "Your tree!"

"Yes. It's been stolen out of my garden, right under my very nose."

"What did it look like?" Sergeant Porter said.

"What did what look like? My nose?"

"Your tree."

"It looked like a tree, of course, you great oaf!" Miss Endicott said. "Don't they teach you anything in the police force? Apart from how to say 'Hello, hello, hello'?"

"They teach us," Sergeant Porter said patiently, "how to solve crimes and arrest criminals. And the first thing we are told to do is to get a good description. So what did this tree look like?"

"Like a tree!" Miss Endicott said. "You know, about twenty feet high, with roots and branches and birds twittering on it, that sort of thing."

"Any squirrels?" Sergeant Porter said as he wrote in his notebook.

"No. But you can't miss it. It's got chimes on it."

"A tree with chimes!" Sergeant Porter said. "A chiming tree! Pull the other one, it's got bells on!"

"Chimes on! Not bells on!" Miss Endicott said, getting hot under the cardigan.

"Chimes. Very well. And did you have your postcode stamped on it?"

"What?"

"Did you have your postcode stamped on your tree, madam?" Sergeant Porter said. "On the trunk?"

"No. I've only got my postcode stamped on my bicycle, not my tree!"

"Well, the police to advise the public to mark their belongings with their postcode. So in future, if I were you, I would mark my tree with my postcode, so that if it's ever stolen and then later found, we will know where to return it. Now, did you see who took this tree?"

"Well, I know it seems a bit unlikely," Miss Endicott said, "but it seemed to me as if the wind took it."

The phone went silent for a moment.

"Wind?" Sergeant Porter said. "Your tree was stolen by—a wind?"

"Yes, a big curly one. It uprooted it, just like that. Disgusting, I call it, great big twisters coming from nowhere and pinching people's trees. You must try and find it. It has great sentimental value. I grew it myself from scratch. In fact I've known that tree since it was just a nut."

"Yes," Sergeant Porter mused. "Just a

nut, eh? Quite a lot of nuts around these days too, if you ask me. Very well, madam, you leave it with us, and we'll see what we can do."

"Good," said Miss Endicott. And she hung up. She looked towards Tiddles and Fido who were still hiding under the sofa.

"It's all right," she said. "You can come out now. That nasty wind's gone."

But just to be on the safe side, they stayed right where they were.

9

Stop That Wind

"The thing to do," Professor Sniff said, as he and Oswald drove after Typhoon Trevor, "is to get it cornered. Once we do that, we can force it down the funnel and get it into the milk churn. Then we stick the top on, get a bit of rope around it, and it's in the bag!"

"Right you are," Oswald said. He looked out of the window as they drove along. Everywhere was in a terrible mess.

"Not very neat, that typhoon, is he?" Oswald said. "He doesn't exactly tidy up after himself. Not what you'd call Tidy Trevor, is he? More like Scruffy Trevor, if you ask me. I just wonder who's going to be expected to pay for all the damage he's done?"

Professor Sniff went pale.

"I hope you're not suggesting that it was *my* fault, Oswald."

"Well, I'm not suggesting it was mine!" Oswald said tetchily.

"It's no one's fault. It's an act of Mother Nature."

"Will Mother Nature pay for the breakages then?" Oswald said.

"Let's not worry about that just now. The important thing is for us to stop it before it does any more damage. So come on."

Typhoon Trevor had been round most of the town, and had left havoc in his wake. He had emptied the outdoor swimming pool and dumped the water on the town hall. He had mixed up all the dustbins for miles, and was using the lids as Frisbees, and seeing how far he could throw them.

A storm warning had gone out, and people were told to stay inside and not to open the door on any account, even if someone banged really hard on the knocker. It seemed that there was nothing anyone could do about the wind, except wait for it to die down.

Not that Trevor showed any signs of dying down. He seemed to get bigger and stronger as he went, as though he were a Pied Piper of winds and breezes. Every little Draught followed him, every stray Gasp and Gulp tagged along. He swelled and grew and swept on his way, and Professor Sniff drove after him, shouting "Turn left, Oswald!" and "Turn right!" and "We'll get him in a minute!"

But Typhoon Trevor was too quick. Whenever they got anywhere near him he just ducked down an alley, or took a back way, or

made a short cut over someone's garden, usually taking their fence with him.

And it wasn't only Professor Sniff who was after him. He was also being chased by the fire brigade, a television news crew, an ambulance and two police cars.

"Stop that wind!" Sergeant Porter yelled. "Take it in for questioning. I have a warrant here for its arrest!"

But Trevor carried on regardless.

Typhoon Trevor took a sharp left into Church Road. Oswald swung the wheel of the truck, and with a squeal of tyres, managed to follow. But the rest of the convoy missed the turn and went driving on.

"Oh no!" said Oswald. "The church! He's going in!"

Typhoon Trevor went inside and zoomed up to the belfry. He rang fourteen o'clock on the bells, just for the hell of it, then zipped down and whooshed out through the church, blowing out all the candles.

He shot into the museum next where he changed all the name cards on the displays. He nipped into the library next, took all the books out, even though he didn't have a ticket, and left them in a heap. He popped into the ten-pin bowling alley and sent all the pins flying. Then he found himself in the ice-cream factory where he whipped a vat of

milk up into one great enormous strawberry milkshake.

"There he goes!" the professor shouted, as a big wave of pink frothy milk came out of the factory windows. "We're gaining on him! Don't stop!"

Typhoon Trevor turned in through the gates of the school. As it was a Saturday, the school was empty, so he zoomed on down to the sports field where a game of football was in progress. Everyone ran to the changing hut when they saw him coming. But he scored three goals anyway, and then went and had a shower, blowing bubbles the size of houses with the soap.

Clean, spruce and smelling fresh, he went on. He turned left, turned right, and the truck was at his heels all the way. He hesitated, got confused, ducked down into Castle Walk and found himself at a dead end. He stopped to get his breath and stood panting.

"Right," said Professor Sniff. "We've got him!"

Oswald stopped the truck, slammed it into reverse, and backed up so that the wide end of the funnel on the trailer faced towards the cornered Trevor.

"Get the milk churn and have the rope ready!" the professor cried. "We haven't a moment to lose!"

They got the milk churn and put the open end of it over the thin end of the funnel.

"OK, the lid's at the ready," said Oswald. "It's all down to him to make his move."

Typhoon Trevor turned to face them.

"Look at him," Oswald said. "He's like a bull, pawing the ground."

But it was impossible to say what Trevor really looked like, as he kept swirling and changing shape. One moment he seemed like a corkscrew, the next he looked like a great enormous genie, who has just escaped from a bottle after years of being corked up.

"Watch out," the professor said, "and hold steady. Here he comes."

Typhoon Trevor faced them angrily. They blocked his route to freedom, and his only way past was to charge and to scatter them aside.

"Make a face," the professor said. "Get him annoyed. That way he won't think straight."

Oswald stuck his tongue out, put his thumb to his nose and waggled his fingers.

"Stupid old Trevor," he said. "Call yourself a typhoon! Hah! I've seen more wind in a baby's bottom. You couldn't even blow a match out!"

At that Trevor rumbled and began to move. He surged forward with all his might, he flew straight ahead, at Oswald and at the professor—

—and straight down into the funnel.

"AOWWWWWWWWW!"

The typhoon seemed to roar with anger and pain. He tried to pull back, but it was too late. He twisted and twirled towards the end of the funnel, crushed under his own energy and speed. It was like the water in a sink, whirling down through the drain. On he went, down into the funnel. And at the far end of it, there were Oswald and the professor, holding on to the milk churn.

"*AOWWWWWWWWW!*"

Trevor felt himself get smaller. Everything went dark. He seemed to be in some small, confined space, smelling ever so slightly of stale milk.

"He's nearly all in, just his tail!"

Trevor managed to turn and look behind him. He saw a spot of daylight back there and headed for it.

"Never mind his tail!" the professor said. "Just slam the lid on. Quick!"

Oswald banged the lid on to the milk churn, and the professor tied it on tightly with the rope. The tail of the typhoon drifted off into the sky, looking lonely and forlorn, like a tail that has lost its dog, and has no one to wag it any more. Then it vanished, like a puff of smoke. "Done it!" Oswald said. "Got him at last!"

10

Tuneless Whistles

The calm before the storm is said to be a strange, eerie thing. But then, in a different way, so too is the calm after it.

"What happened?" people said. 'It's gone quiet! You could hear a pin drop—if you had one—and dropped it."

"Where's that wind gone? Did anyone see where it went?"

"Never mind that, where'd it come from?"

But nobody had seen anything. And nobody paid much attention to the truck and trailer with the roped-up milk churn on it as Professor Sniff and Oswald drove by, and out of town.

In their flat, Sam and Lorna looked out of the window.

"It's stopped, Dad," Lorna said.

"Yes," said Sam. "Shall we go back out and try to fly the kite again?"

"No," said Dad. "Let's not." And he seemed quite definite about it.

Professor Sniff and Oswald took Typhoon Trevor back to the wind farm, and locked him up, still in the milk churn, in a strong corrugated-iron shed with triple padlocks.

"What now, Professor?" Oswald said.

"Well," said the professor, "I think maybe we'd better lie low for a while, and act all innocent. Let's go and get ourselves a few Tuneless Whistles from the store. Tuneless Whistles are always good for acting innocent when there's been trouble."

"Tuneless Whistles it is then," said Oswald. And he went to get them.

Typhoon Trevor had left the town in an awful mess.

Nothing was where it should have been. Traffic lights had been uprooted, caravans and even whole houses had been moved. People who used to live at number 23, now found that their house had moved to number 78. And people from number 78 found themselves living in a different street entirely. Sam and Lorna's dustbin had disappeared, and it was posted back to them six weeks later by someone living in Africa.

Once the storm was over, Miss Endicott clipped Tiddles's lead on to his collar, and the two of them went down to the police station. Sergeant Porter saw them coming, but it was too late to hide.

"Shop!" she said. "I want a bit of attention. Now! Lost property! Have you had a tree handed in yet?"

"Oh, yes. Hang on," Sergeant Porter said. "I'll check the books."

"Check the trees, never mind the books!"

Sergeant Porter opened the lost-property ledger. "Yes," he said, "oddly enough, we have had several trees handed in since the small outbreak of bad weather."

"How many?" Miss Endicott said.

"Eight hundred and two," he said. "Plus a bulldozer, nine hundred cars, forty cats, seventeen lawn-mowers, eighty garden sheds, two dozen snails, a polar bear, seven crabs, a donkey—oh, and a frog called Nigel."

"Well, you can't miss my tree," Miss Endicott said. "It's got wind chimes on it. And it answers to the name of Doris."

"I never heard of trees," Sergeant Porter said, "ever answering to the name of anything. But if you care to go out the back, we have all the trees in the yard. If you can recognize yours, you can take it home."

Miss Endicott and Tiddles went out to the yard at the back of the police station where crowds of people were milling around looking for their belongings.

"There it is!" Miss Endicott said. "My tree!

I'd recognize it anywhere. I never forget a branch." She went to her tree and gave it a cuddle, and they were very glad to be reunited. And Tiddles seemed quite pleased to see it too.

"Come along, Doris," Miss Endicott said, "let's go home and replant you." She turned to Sergeant Porter, who had followed her outside.

"Maybe this nice man will give us a lift."

"You'll have to get a taxi," Sergeant Porter said. "Or take it on the bus. It's not the police's job to go giving lifts home to trees."

So Miss Endicott had to call for a cab.

"It's a bit big," the driver said, "but if I open the sun roof, it might fit in." And it did, so he drove them all home. He even helped Miss Endicott carry her tree round to the back garden, and they dropped it back into its hole.

"Good as new!" the driver said.

"Thank you," Miss Endicott said. "You must let me give you a tip. Never go swimming with lead boots on. Now that's a good tip, isn't it?"

"Very," the driver said. "Very useful."

"And here's five pounds for your trouble too," she said.

"I haven't got any trouble," the driver told her.

"I'd better have it back then," she said.

"On second thoughts," the taxi driver said, "I might have some trouble after all."

Some days later, Oswald and Professor Sniff were busy on the wind farm, mucking out the Gasps.

"I expect everyone in the town'll be wondering who's going to pay for the damage that typhoon did," Oswald said casually, with an eye on the professor.

Professor Sniff moved uneasily.

"I should think that the word on everyone's lips down in the town right now is *compensation*," Oswald went on. "A bit of damage, a bit of compensation. That's how folks' minds work."

Professor Sniff looked towards the shed, where the typhoon was locked up.

"Yes, I've been thinking about that, Oswald," he said. "And I may have a way of making it up to people. Maybe a little treat of some sort."

"That's good," Oswald said. "Treats. I always like the sound of them. And what about that Typhoon Trevor? What are we going to do with him?"

"That," Professor Sniff said, "is all part of the plan."

"Then I can't wait to hear it," Oswald said.

"Bring that milk churn over to the processing plant, Oswald," Professor Sniff said. "And we'll get cracking. And make it snappy."

"Snappy cracking, eh?" Oswald said. "Sounds all right to me."

11

Pesky Draughts and a Big Stinky

Oswald and Professor Sniff worked through the night. Mrs Sniff brought them frequent cups of tea and slices of her famous sponge cake.

"Light as a sunbeam, that sponge cake, my dear," the professor said.

"It's all thanks to your Light As A Feather Best Baking Bubbles, my love," Mrs Sniff said. "For it's not just the mixture, it's the quality of air."

Professor Sniff took the milk churn with the typhoon inside, and dropped it into the feeder of his wind machine, pulling off the lid as he did so.

Free again, Typhoon Trevor shot off down the tubes into the processing plant, looking for a means of escape.

But there was none. The only way to go was

straight ahead, down into the processor.

WHOOSH! PARFF! SCROOM!

The professor touched a lever here, a button there, he adjusted a handle, he tapped a gauge.

"How are we doing?" he said.

"Steady as she goes," Oswald said. "What should I set the dial for?"

"Set it for Burps," the professor said.

Oswald reached for a dial marked Output and he set it to Burps.

"Quantity?" he asked.

"How many people live in the town?"

"About ten thousand. Give or take."

"Set it for twenty thousand," the professor said. "That's two each."

The processing plant rattled and groaned as it turned the typhoon into a heap of Burps, which poured out of the other end, along the conveyor belt.

"Easy as we go. Don't want them bursting."

"What now?" Oswald asked. "There's plenty of wind left."

"How about a few Sighs?" the professor answered.

"Contented Sighs? Or Sighs of Relief?"

"Contented, I think," the professor said. "Two each again." And Oswald set the dial to Sighs, Type 3.

The great wind-processing machine ground into action. And this time a quantity of Sighs came out of the delivery chute and chugged along the conveyor to the packaging machine.

"Still plenty of wind left," Oswald said. "What now?"

"Two Chinese Whispers each," the professor replied.

And Oswald set the dial for Whispers, Chinese.

"Then how about a Good Parp for everyone," he suggested, "and some Nice Cooling Breezes, for blowing the cobwebs away."

The professor nodded, so Oswald turned the dial, and hit the button.

"And how about a few Sweet Nothings?" he said. "Very fond of Sweet Nothings, folk are. I know there's nothing to them, but they are sweet. There's nothing like a Sweet Nothing whispered in your ear. Especially from the one you love."

"Good idea," the professor said. "Sweet Nothings it is."

Sweet Nothings, Good Sneezes, Second Winds, there were two of each for everyone. Little by little the wind-processing machine turned the typhoon into small and useful parts.

"And how about two Pesky Draughts each to finish with?" Oswald said. "Just for fun?"

"Pesky Draughts it is, Oswald," the

professor said, and he set the dial himself. And the last of Typhoon Trevor was used up.

They loaded up the trailer, and went into town while it was still dark.

On every doorstep, they left a bag of goodies, and a note saying:

Sorry for the recent bad weather.
Please accept this small gift.
With our compliments.

At Sam and Lorna Walker's house, it was Lorna who found the package, when she went to bring in the milk.

"Mum, look," she said. "Someone left this by the door. What is it?"

"Free samples of some sort," Mum said. "Let's see."

She opened the package, reached inside and took out a small, clear bubble, made from some kind of film. A label attached to it read "Cooling Breeze. Pinch Open For Immediate Relief."

Mum pinched the bubble. It split, and the most refreshing, cooling breeze she had ever known came out and blew softly around her face.

"Good heavens! How beautifully relaxing. I feel ten years younger."

"Let's have one then," Dad said. "I want to feel ten years younger too."

"And me!" Lorna said.

"Lorna," Mum said, "If you were ten years younger, you wouldn't even exist. Ten years ago, you were just a gleam in your father's eye."

Lorna looked at her dad to see if his eyes had any more gleams in them that might one day turn into brothers or sisters. But she didn't know if she could see any or not.

Mum looked into the bag and gave Lorna and Sam a Good Sneeze each to play with.

"Only open them over by the window!"

They broke them open.

"*Atchoo!*"

"*Atchoo!*"

"Steady," Dad said. "You'll have the table over."

"What a sneeze!" Lorna said.

"Terrific!" Sam said. "Did you see that? I went and sneezed the cat into the garden!"

"And I sneezed the postman over, did you see?"

"Oi! Be careful," the postman called from the pavement, getting back on to his feet.

"What else is in there, Dad?" Sam asked. "Let's see." He peered into the bag and took out another bubble.

"Oh look, Pesky Draughts. There's one each. Can we have them? It says they're Non-Toxic, Long-Lasting, and Ideal For Children."

"All right," Mum said. "One Pesky Draught each, then it's school."

*

Over at Miss Endicott's house, it was Fido who found the package on the doorstep, just as he was coming out of his cat flap to take the morning air.

"Meow!" he went.

"What's that cat on about now?" Miss Endicott said, and went to see.

"Meow," Fido said, and he pointed at the package with his paw.

Miss Endicott took the parcel indoors and opened it.

"Now, what have we here?" she said, taking out a Proper Snort and looking at it. Fido jumped up on to her lap and dug his sharp claws into it.

Snooooooort!!

The cat fell off the chair in fright, and ran away to hide in the bread bin. Luckily there was no bread in it, as Miss Endicott kept her bread in the washing machine. She had forgotten where it was supposed to go, and had put it in there for safe keeping. Her washing was in the fridge. It didn't get very clean in there, but it stayed nice and cool.

"Oh my! That certainly was a Proper Snort,

wasn't it? Now, what else have we? A Good Burp? I haven't had a Good Burp in ages. And what else, I wonder?" She took out a large bubble inside which strange yellow smoke curled. She peered at the label.

"A Big Stinky," she read. "I wonder what a Big Stinky is, Fido? Shall we open it?"

But Fido decided that he didn't want to find out what a Big Stinky was, and he jumped down from the bread bin and was off out of his cat flap before Miss Endicott could open it. She popped it with a knitting needle.

Pop!

And the most awful smell filled the room and she had to open all the windows. The smell was still there an hour later, when her friend Miss Bayliss came to visit.

"Good heavens," she said. "What's that terrible pong?"

"Well, it wasn't *me*!" Miss Endicott said. "It was my Big Stinky."

So the day passed. And people were so delighted with their packages they forgot all about the typhoon and the damage it had done.

Gentle Breezes played about their ears all day. Everywhere you went you could hear someone having a Good Sneeze or a Proper Belch or a Decent Burp—as though they hadn't had such things in a long time.

Sam and Lorna played with their Pesky Draughts all day. And many other children brought theirs to school too. The Draughts annoyed the teacher no end, as they kept rustling her papers, and blowing the door open.

"Where are all those Pesky Draughts coming from?" she said.

But nobody answered. They just took out their Tuneless Whistles, and tried to look as innocent as they could.

Even Sergeant Porter at the police station got his bag of goodies from the wind farm. He put a Cooling Breeze under his helmet, and it kept him happy all day.

Professor and Mrs Sniff drove down into the town later in the evening, to check how people were getting on, and to see if all was forgiven.

Everywhere they went, they heard the same thing. Gentle Snores came from the children's bedrooms. In the living rooms, where their parents were still awake, they could hear the sound of Sweet Nothings being whispered into ears. And these were followed by Affectionate Murmurs, and then later by Soppy Kisses and Contented Sighs as the lights went out, one by one.

"It's a funny old business, the wind business," Professor Sniff said. "But there's no other business like it. And I wouldn't do anything else, my dear, because it's the only business I know."

The last light went out. The town fell silent, save for the odd Snore and Snurkle.

"Feel that, my dear?" Mrs Sniff said, as a gentle wind ruffled her hair. "I do believe the spring breezes are here."

"Yes," Professor Sniff said. "I do believe they are."

And the breezes clustered round him, like his long-lost friends. And when he drove back to the wind farm, they followed him home like lambs.

"Yes, it's an ill wind," the professor said, "that blows no one any good."

And when he wasn't looking, Mrs Sniff leaned over, and she gave him a big Soppy Kiss, one that she herself had prepared earlier. And it was really rather a nice one too. Not that Professor Sniff would ever admit it.

If you've enjoyed *Professor Sniff and the Lost Spring Breezes* you might also like the other 'Callender Hill' stories by Alex Shearer. Lorna and Sam, Miss Endicott and Tiddles the dog continue their hilarious seasonal adventures in *The Summer Sisters and the Dance Disaster* and, coming shortly, *Dr Twilite and the Autumn Snooze* and *The Winter Brothers and the Missing Snow*.